## Basketball Legends

# Ben Simmons

First published by Albert Street Books, an imprint of Allen & Unwin, in 2024



Allen & Unwin
Cammeraygal Country
83 Alexander Street
Crows Nest NSW 2065
Australia
Phone: (61 2) 8425 0100
Email: info@allenandunwin.com
Web: www.allenandunwin.com

*Allen & Unwin acknowledges the Traditional Owners of the Country on which we live and work. We pay our respects to all Aboriginal and Torres Strait Islander Elders, past and present.*

A catalogue record for this book is available from the National Library of Australia

ISBN 978 1 76118 127 6

For teaching resources, explore allenandunwin.com/learn

Cover design by Hana Kinoshita Thomson
Cover photo by The Canadian Press / Alamy Stock Photo
Text design by Hana Kinoshita Thomson
Set in 14 pt Urbane Rounded Medium
Printed and bound in Australia by the Opus Group



10 9 8 7 6 5 4 3 2 1

BASKETBALL LEGENDS

# BEN SIMMONS

KIT CROSS

LEIGH HEDSTROM

ALBERT STREET BOOKS

# CONTENTS

# BEN IS AWESOME

Hi, there. I'm Gary, your friendly neighbourhood goat.

I like to call myself the **G.G.O.A.T. (Greatest Gatherer of Outstanding Athletic Trivia).**

Don't mix that up with the **G.O.A.T. (Greatest of All Time)** though! I'm just a regular goat.

But you know who *is* a

# REAL LIFE LEGEND?

Basketball player

## BEN SIMMONS

And this book is all about him!

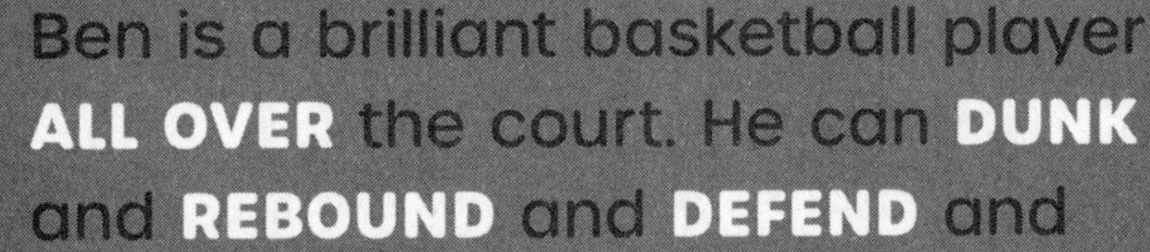

Ben is a brilliant basketball player **ALL OVER** the court. He can **DUNK** and **REBOUND** and **DEFEND** and

**MAKE PLAY.**

Ben is **so good** that in **2016,** he became the

THIRD AUSTRALIAN EVER

to have been the **NUMBER ONE**

*first overall draft pick*

in the **NBA.** He was also the **first Aussie** to win

**ROOKIE OF THE YEAR**

in his **first season.**

What makes Ben such a

# LEGEND

on the court?

## ATHLETICISM

Ben is **strong, quick** and **agile.** For a big, tall guy, he can really move!

## VERSATILITY

His usual position is **point guard,** but Ben is dangerous wherever he plays – **up forward** or in **defence.**

## REBOUNDS

Ben is

**brilliant**

on the boards, **retrieving the ball** when the other team misses a shot.

## DECISION MAKING

He is a **super smart player** who reads the play well and **stays one step ahead** of the game.

Overhead pass

Dunk

Defence

Three-point shot

Layup

Crossover dribble

Jump shot

Rebound

'If you try to veer him one way or another, he's **too big and strong.** He'll get through that. He makes passes. He makes plays. **He's coming in with a lot of confidence.'**

**JEFF HORNACEK,** head coach of the New York Knicks

**Name:**
Benjamin David Simmons

**Date of Birth:**
20 July 1996

**Place of Birth:**
Fitzroy, VIC

**Height:**
2.08m

**Position:**
Point guard

**Number:**
10

**Nicknames:**
Benny, The Wizard of Oz, Fresh Prince, Big Ben

**Teams:** LSU Tigers, Philadelphia 76ers, Brooklyn Nets

# TALL TALES

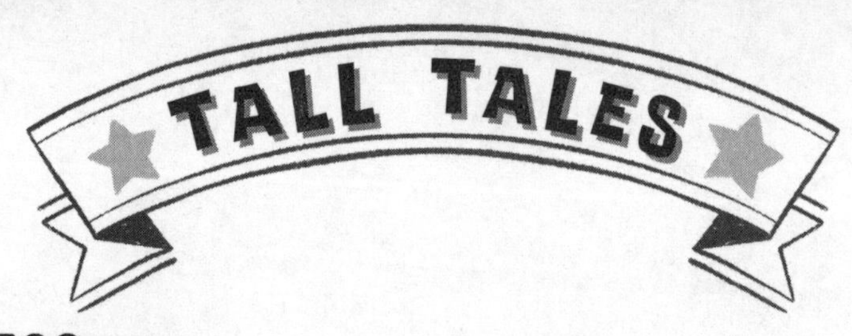

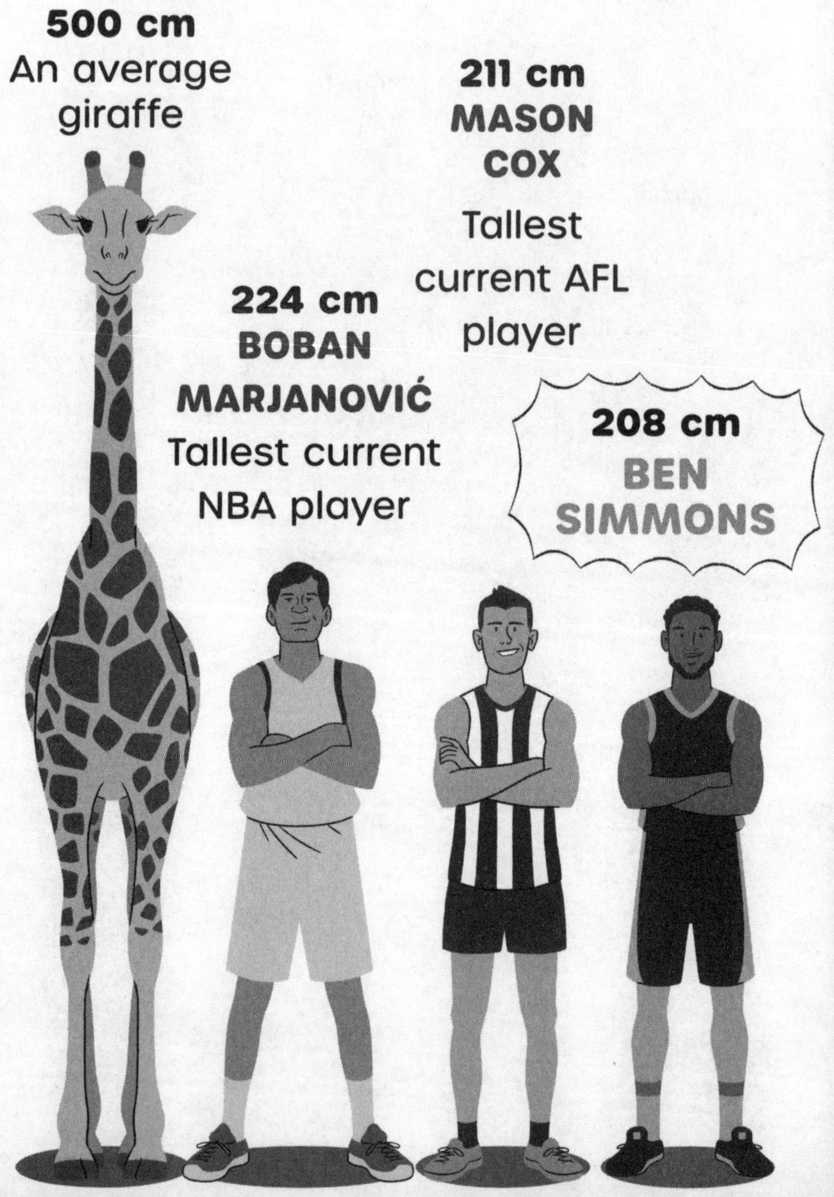

500 cm
An average giraffe
224 cm
BOBAN MARJANOVIĆ
Tallest current NBA player
211 cm
MASON COX
Tallest current AFL player
208 cm
BEN SIMMONS

**206 cm**
**LIZ CAMBAGE**
Legendary Australian WNBA player

**181 cm**
**MACKENZIE ARNOLD**
Tallest current Matildas player

**170 cm**
**LIONEL MESSI**
Legendary Argentinian soccer player

**104 cm**
**ZEUS**
The world's tallest dog (he's a Great Dane)

**BEN SIMMONS,**

aged 13

# AUSSIE, AUSSIE, AUSSIE

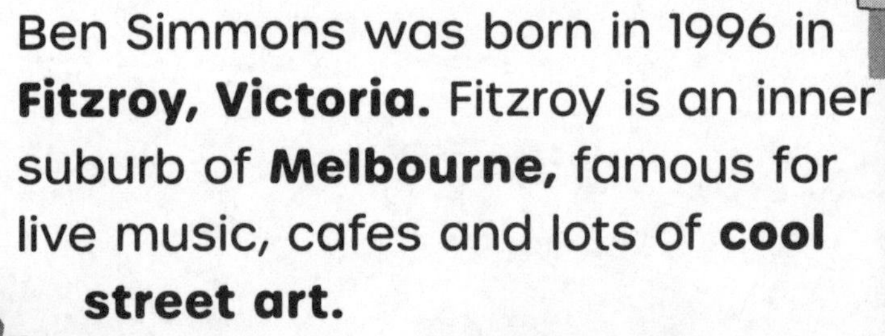

Ben Simmons was born in 1996 in **Fitzroy, Victoria.** Fitzroy is an inner suburb of **Melbourne,** famous for live music, cafes and lots of **cool street art.**

A popular piece is the huge mural of the **Harlem Globetrotters basketball team!**

Did you know there are street art murals of Ben in Melbourne as well?

Ben comes from a **sporty family.** His **dad** was an **amazing basketballer** too!

**Dave Simmons** was born in America but moved to Australia in the late 1980s to play for the **Melbourne Tigers NBL team.**

In his **first game** with the Tigers, Dave scored **28 points** and became a **big favourite** with the fans!

So it's **not surprising** that Ben grew up **playing basketball.**

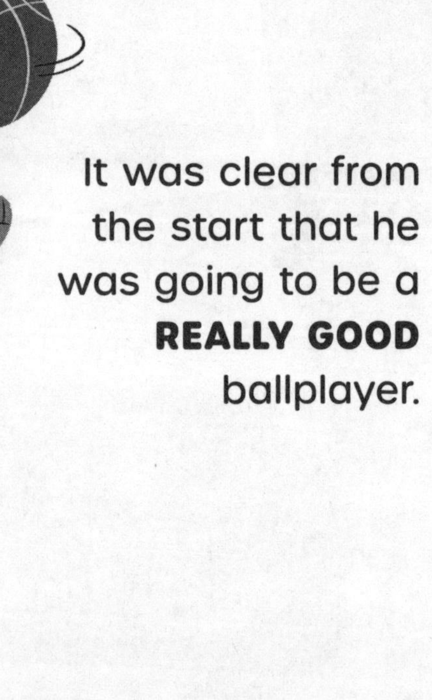

It was clear from the start that he was going to be a **REALLY GOOD** ballplayer.

But as a kid he played a lot of **other sports** – he loved **rugby** and **AFL,** too.

‘He was an **absolute freak.**

He could **jump.** He could **run.**

He honestly would have been a

**top-five draft pick**

if he had stuck with football.’

**CHRISTIAN PETRACCA,**
AFL player

Ben and Christian
(who plays for the
MELBOURNE
DEMONS and is a bit
of a legend himself!) were
CO-CAPTAINS of the
Victorian Primary Schools
basketball team, and
they played junior
footy together.

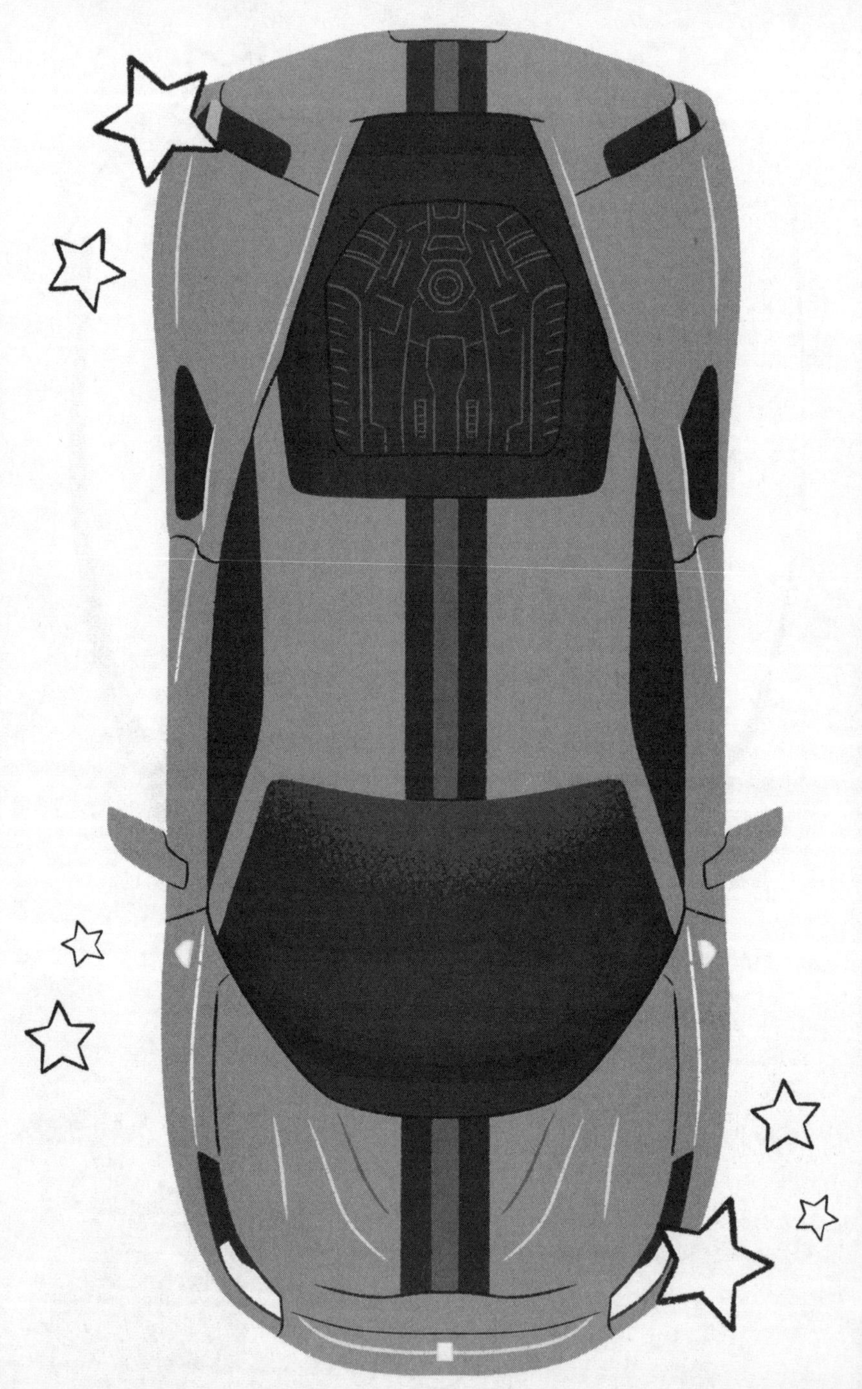

Ben lives in the USA now, but he must be a **Melbourne boy** at heart because he had a **Ferrari** custom built for him in **red, black and grey** – the colours of his favourite AFL club, the **Essendon Bombers.**

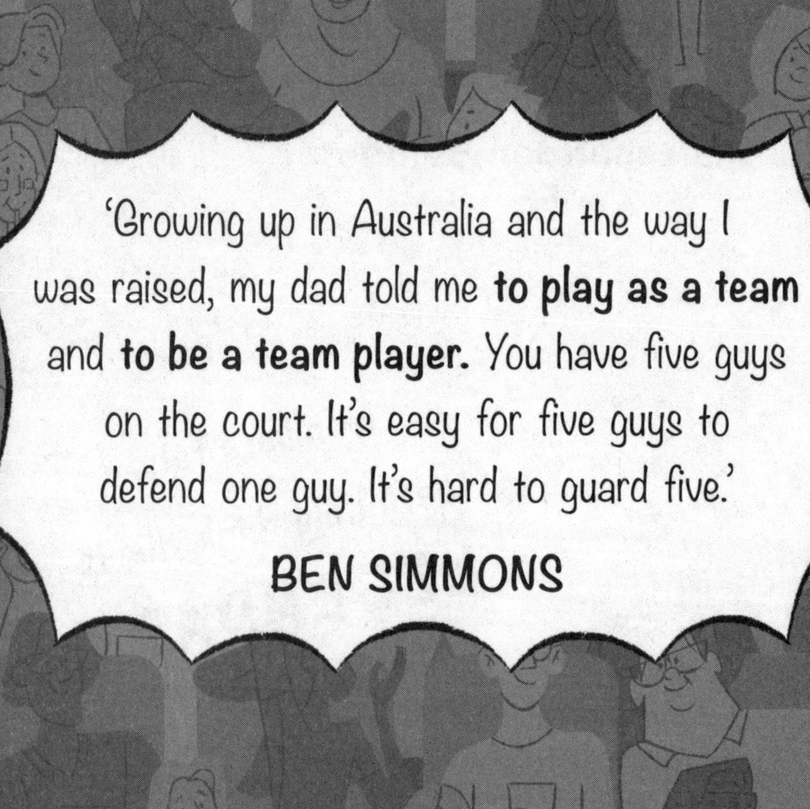

'Growing up in Australia and the way I was raised, my dad told me **to play as a team** and **to be a team player.** You have five guys on the court. It's easy for five guys to defend one guy. It's hard to guard five.'

BEN SIMMONS

## CHAPTER THREE

# THE EARLY DAYS

Ben was just **seven years old** when he started playing for the **Newcastle Hunters Under 12s** basketball team.

When he was **ten,** he and his family returned to **Melbourne** and Ben joined the

He played for his high school

and for the

SOUTH-EAST EAGLES

helping them with the

**under 16s premiership.**

Aussie tennis **legend** **PAT CASH** also went to school at Whitefriars, nearly **30 years before** Ben was there.

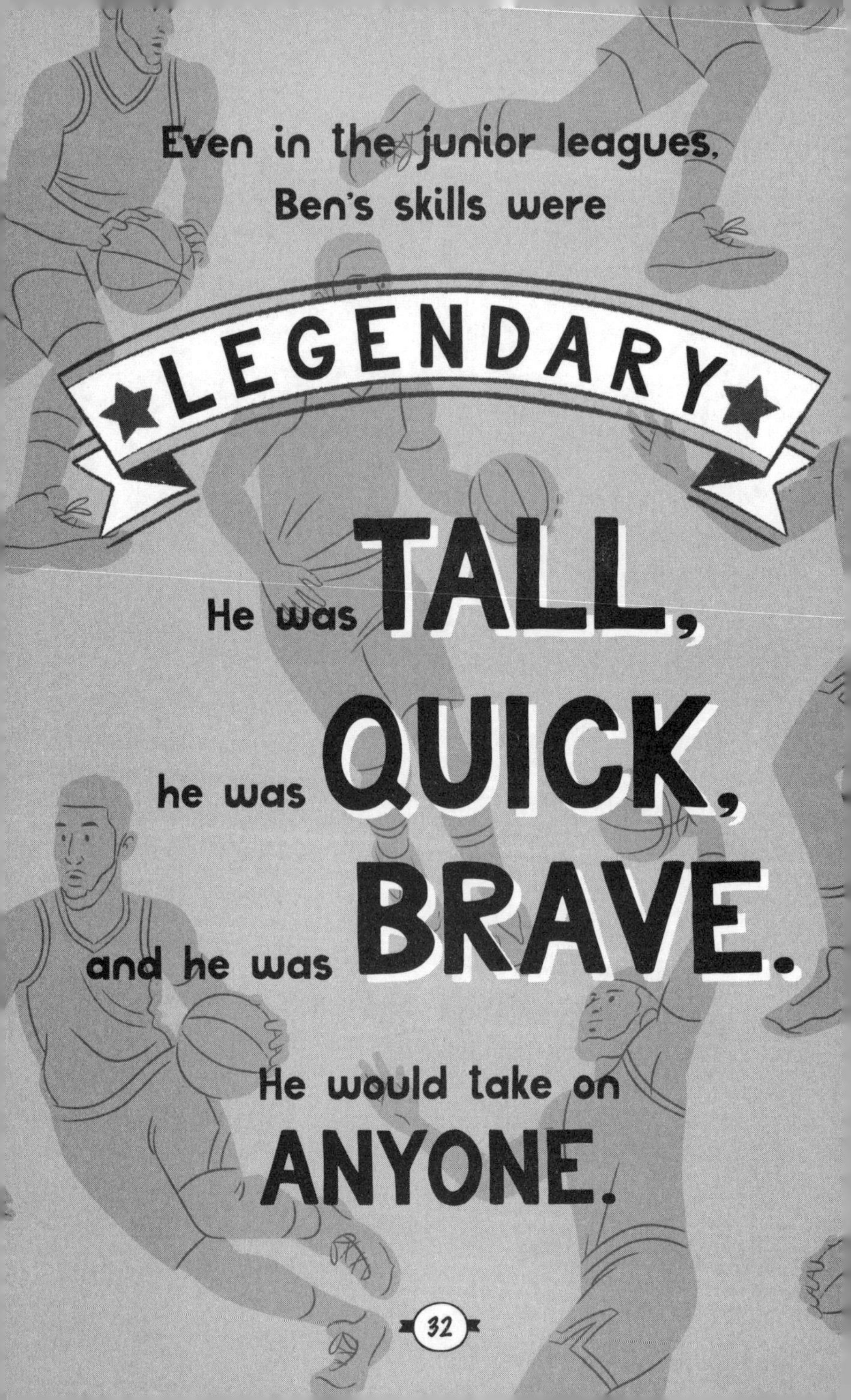

Even in the junior leagues,
Ben's skills were

LEGENDARY

He was **TALL**,

he was **QUICK**,

and he was **BRAVE**.

He would take on
**ANYONE**.

Ben 'could **get down the court and dunk** in the under 16s, he was a **great shooter**, he was basically the **perfect all-round player** for a 15-year-old athlete.'

**NATHAN SEWELL,**
Knox Basketball committee member

Ben was **so good at basketball** that the principal of Box Hill Senior Secondary College agreed to create a whole **new basketball program** at the school, just so Ben would play with them!

He went on to play at the **2011 Australian Schools Championships** for Box Hill SCC.

‘I thought he could be one of the **best players** this country’s ever produced…’

**KEVIN GOORJIAN,** head basketball coach of Box Hill Senior Secondary College

Ben might have been **naturally talented,** but he still had a lot of skills to **learn** and **practise:**

# CHAPTER FOUR

# FACTS ABOUT STATS

If you already know **ALL ABOUT basketball statistics,** you can skip to page 45!

**Tracking stats** help players, commentators, coaches and fans **track the progress** of a team and individual players across a game, or a tournament, or a whole career!

# FIVE MAIN CATEGORIES

★ POINTS ★

★ REBOUNDS ★

★ ASSISTS ★

★ STEALS ★

★ BLOCKS ★

When a player reaches **double figures (10 or higher)** in any **two** of those main categories in **one game,** they have achieved a

FOR EXAMPLE:
26 points + 12 rebounds
**= DOUBLE-DOUBLE**

If they get to **double figures** in THREE of the categories in one match, it is called a

# TRIPLE-DOUBLE

FOR EXAMPLE:

27 points + 15 rebounds + 13 assists

**= TRIPLE-DOUBLE**

Triple-doubles are almost always **points, rebounds and assists.** They are quite rare in a game, and Ben Simmons is a **triple-double legend!**

# Some terms

**PPG**
Points Per Game

**RPG**
Rebounds Per Game

**SPG**
Steals Per Game

**BPG**
Blocks Per Game

**3PT%**
Percentage of three-point shots

# to remember

**PER GAME** stats are an **average** worked out using maths. The **equation** looks like this:

Number of points scored by number of games played = Points Per Game

**FOR EXAMPLE:**
30 points ÷ 6 games = 5 PPG

There is also a **statistic** you sometimes see called the **Player Efficiency Rating [PER].**

The first equation you have to do looks like this:

$$uPER = \frac{1}{min} \times \left(3P + \left[\frac{2}{3} \times AST\right]\right.$$

$$+ \left[\left(2 - factor \times \frac{tmAST}{tmFG}\right) \times FG\right]$$

$$+ \left[0.5 \times FT \times \left(2 - \frac{1}{3} \times \frac{tmAST}{tmFG}\right)\right] - [VOP \times TO]$$

# FROM PLAY TIME TO THE BIG TIME

'I'm the best **PlayStation player** you'll ever see. **I'll play anything.** *Call of Duty, NBA2K, Grand Theft Auto.*'

**BEN SIMMONS**

One of Ben's best mates is **Dante Exum,** another **Australian NBA legend** from Melbourne, who now plays for the **Dallas Mavericks.**

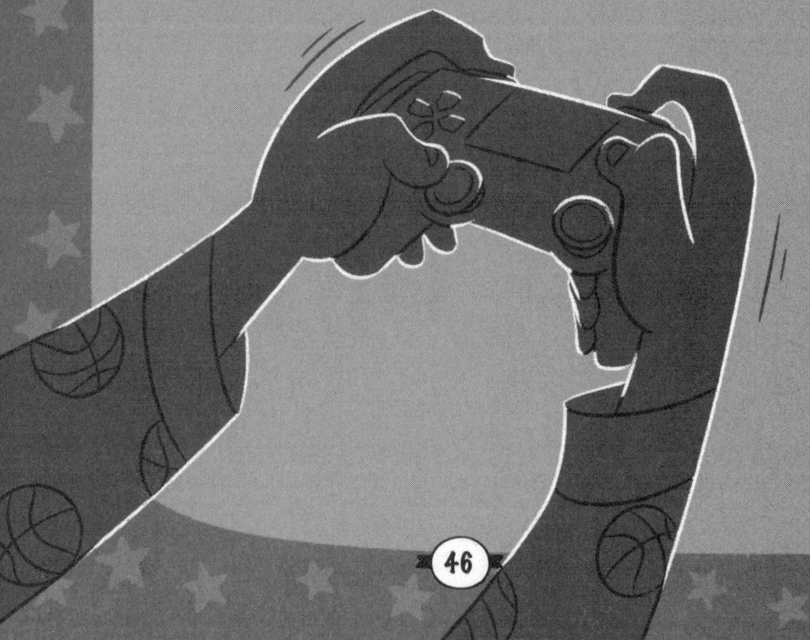

**Ben** and **Dante** used to go to each other's houses after basketball practice...**and stay up all night** playing video games!

**I bet their parents thought this was NOT legendary behaviour!**

But the late nights can't have been so bad, because in **2012,** when he was just **fifteen years old,** Ben won a **scholarship** to the

AUSTRALIAN INSTITUTE OF SPORT

The **AIS** is a **high-performance sports training facility,** where athletes get intensive coaching in **SKILLS, MINDSET** and **FITNESS.** In other words, it's a **legend factory!**

# AIS LEGENDS

**Ricky Ponting**
Captain and coach of the Australian Cricket Team

**Anna Meares**
Olympic gold medal cyclist

**Lauren Jackson**
WNBA superstar

**Michael Klim**
Olympic gold medal swimmer

★AIS★
Ben only spent **one year** at the AIS. But during that year he was chosen to represent Australia in the **2012 FIBA Under 17s World Cup.**
At 15 he was a year younger than almost ALL the other players – how cool!

# TOURNAMENT STATS

**Points Per Game**

(PPG): **9**

**Rebounds Per Game**

(RPG): **5.4**

**Assists Per Game**

(APG): **1.1**

# LEGENDARY GAME

## WHAT?

2012 FIBA Under 17s World Cup semifinal

## WHO?

Australia vs Czech Republic

## WHERE?

Lithuania

## Why was it LEGENDARY?

Ben made **26 points, 10 rebounds** and **5 steals,** leading to Australia **winning 83-71!**

The Australian team came **second in the tournament,** only losing to the USA in the final.

Ben's mate **Dante Exum** was on the team too!

After his year at the AIS, Ben left Australia and **moved to the USA.**

In America, he could get **A LOT** more experience playing other really **good athletes his own age.**

He would also be closer to the centre of **basketball culture** and could catch the attention of **college basketball scouts.**

'I thought it was a long way to go for someone so young.'
**Julie,** Ben's mum

Ben headed to **Florida** – home of alligators, beautiful beaches and Disney World – to go to **Montverde Academy.**

Montverde is famous for its **elite basketball program,** and the team Ben played for there is called the **MONTVERDE EAGLES.**

Ben played for the Eagles for **three years,** helping them **win back-to-back titles** at the High School National Tournament.

# TROPHY CABINET

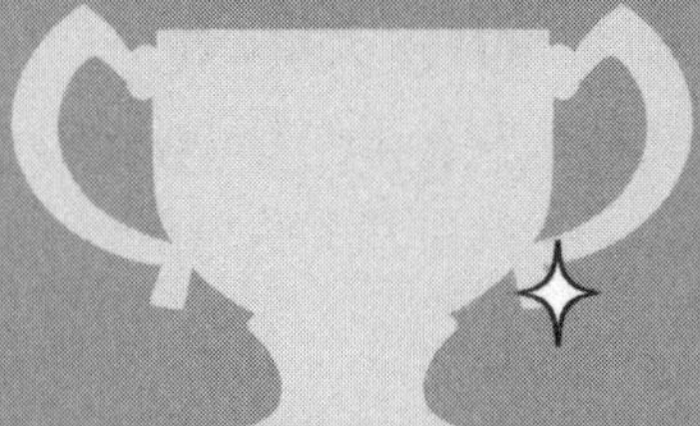

America's Top High School Junior

Voted MVP at the National Basketball Players Association Top 100 Camp

ESPN's #1 Power Forward

ESPN's #1 High School Player in the Nation

Naismith Prep Player of the Year

## – HIGH SCHOOL

**Morgan Wootten National Player of the Year Award***

**Gatorade National Player of the Year**

*LeBron James also won this one!

In his senior year (that's what they call **Year 12** in America), Ben played **29 regular season games,** averaging...

**28 points**

**11.9 rebounds**

**4.0 assists**

**2.6 steals**

He posted 24 DOUBLE-DOUBLES that year!

By the end of high school, Ben had his sights firmly set on joining the
NATIONAL BASKETBALL ASSOCIATION.

# ONE AND DONE

The **NBA** is the highest professional basketball **league for men** in America, and the **WNBA** is the highest professional **league for women.**

# Some NBA and WNBA LEGENDS

Michael Jordan

Kobe Bryant

Diana Taurasi

Charles Barkley

Lauren Jackson
(an Aussie!)

But the **NBA has a rule** designed to help **protect and develop young athletes:**

- You can't join the league straight out of high school.

To be **eligible for the draft** you have to:

- Be at least 19 years old.
- Be at least one full year out of high school.

This is sometimes called the

## ONE and DONE rule

because after **ONE year** you are **DONE** and you can **join the NBA draft.**

You don't have to go to **university,** but **most young athletes choose to,** so they can play basketball for a **college team** and hopefully attract the attention of **NBA scouts.**

When Ben **graduated** from Montverde Academy, he decided to go to **Louisiana State University,** and join the **LSU Tigers.**

The state of **Louisiana** is right next to Florida, and is known for hot, humid weather, delicious **Cajun food,** and **jazz music.**

During his time at uni, Ben was known for **loving basketball,** but for not being very happy about **having to study at the same time.**

Ben's college stats were

– the best any player had achieved in **20 years!**

19.2 PPG

11.8 RBP

4.8 APG

President Barack Obama even gave Ben a shout-out when he visited LSU!

'You got an OK basketball player named Ben Simmons in the house?'
Barack Obama, president of the USA

# LEGENDARY GAME

**WHAT?** 2015 college basketball tournament

**WHO?** LSU Tigers vs North Florida Ospreys

**WHERE?** Baton Rouge, Louisiana

**WHY WAS IT LEGENDARY?**

Ben made 43 points, 14 rebounds, 7 assists, 3 blocks, 5 steals and 2 turnovers!

'I've never seen a more talented dude than Durant, but this dude (Simmons) guards. This dude **rebounds;** this guy gets **steals** and his **IQ is off the roof,** and I've never seen a more **complete package** than this particular person. His **overall game** and his **overall talent** is as great as I've ever seen. Wow.'

**MATTHEW DRISCOLL,**
head coach of
North Florida Ospreys

# Things BEN

- Sneakers
- Playing *Call of Duty*
- Fast cars

# SIMMONS loves

- Playing pool 
- The Essendon football club
- Animals

After his **one year at university** was over, Ben decided that the life of a student was not for him. **He declared himself ready for the NBA draft.**

# ALL THE WAY TO THE NBA

is a big event held **once a year,** where teams can pick **brand new players.** Teams take it in turns to choose.

The teams that didn't do very well in the previous season get to **pick first,** so that they get **first shot** at the **best players.** This is meant to **even up the competition.**

Ben **declared** for the **draft** in **2016.**

His skills were already so

that the

used the **first pick** of the **very first round** to select...

FIRST OVERALL DRAFT PICK! WHAT A LEGEND!

Did you know that **Melbourne, Australia** has produced more **Number 1 draft picks** than any other city in the world??

More than Chicago!
More than LA!
More than New York!

- 2005 - Andrew Bogut
- 2011 - Kyrie Irving*
- 2016 - Ben Simmons

*Kyrie moved to the USA when he was only two years old, but we're still counting him!

Melbourne: legendary basketball town, apparently!

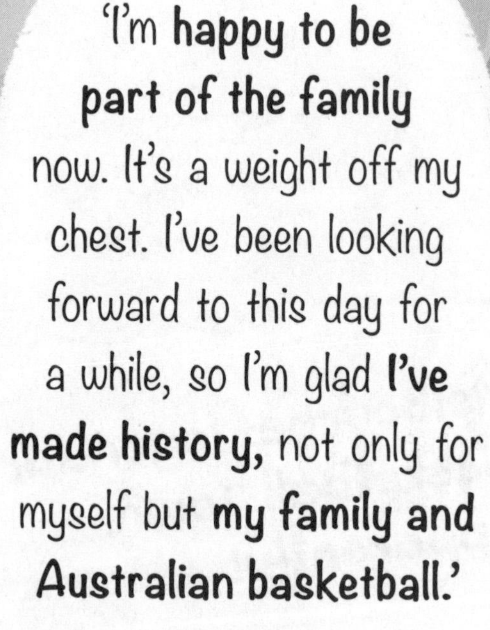

'I'm **happy to be part of the family** now. It's a weight off my chest. I've been looking forward to this day for a while, so I'm glad **I've made history,** not only for myself but **my family and Australian basketball.'**

**BEN SIMMONS,**
on his selection by the 76ers

# PHILADELPHIA DAYS

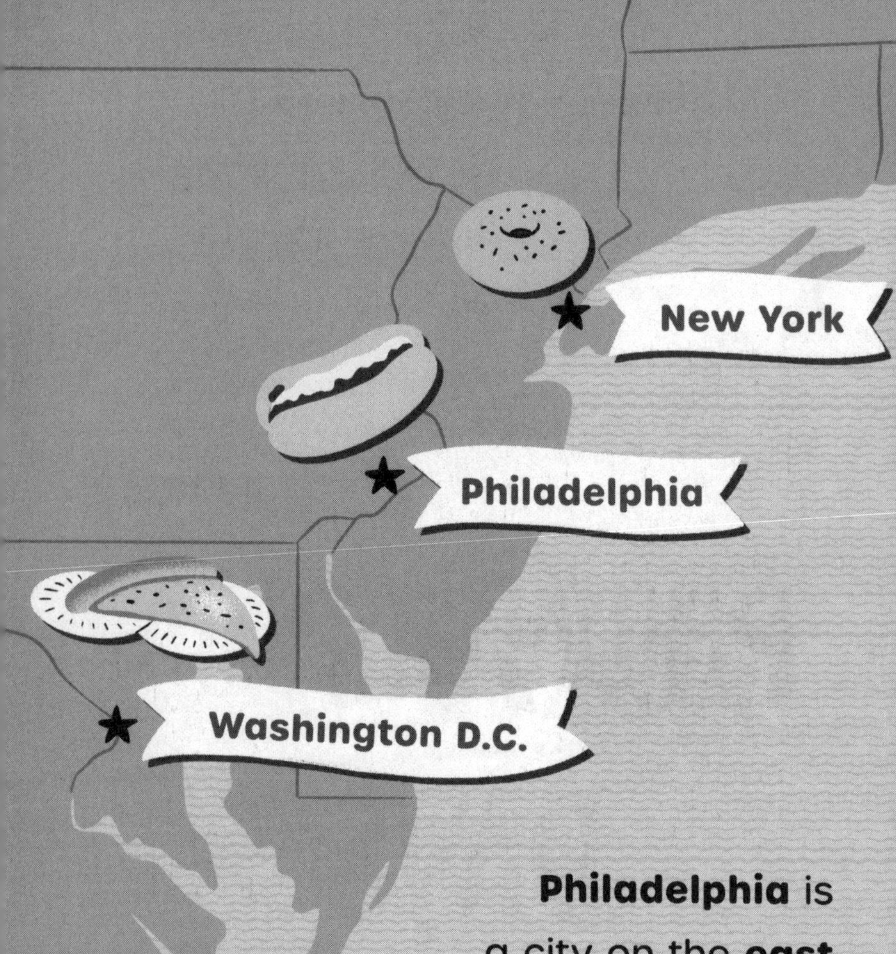


**Philadelphia** is a city on the **east coast** of the **USA,** halfway between **New York** and **Washington D.C.**

**Philly** is the home of cheesesteaks, Will Smith and the **76ers basketball team.**

They are called **the 76ers** because the **Declaration of Independence** was signed there in **1776.** But mostly people just call them **the Sixers.**

Before he could play his first game for the Sixers, **Ben injured his foot** at a **training camp** and had to **sit out** the whole season.

Ben had **fractured a bone** in his right foot and had to have **surgery** to **repair** it. What a

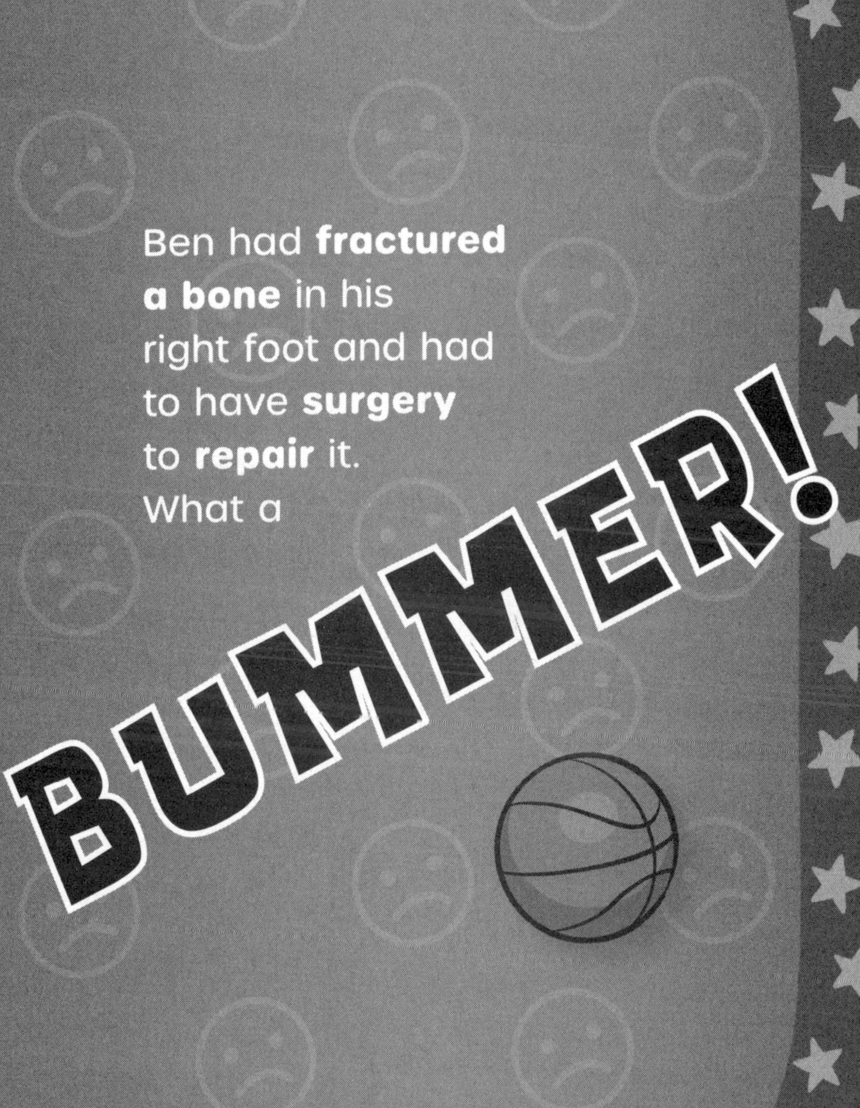

But after the **injury healed,** Ben was **more than ready** for the court! His first season of playing with **the Sixers** was **AMAZING.**

He scored...

**TWELVE TRIP**

LE-DOUBLES

That's the second-most by any rookie in the history of the NBA!

In his **first season,**
in **81 games** Ben averaged:

**15.8 points**

**8.2 assists**

**8.1 rebounds**

PLUS, he won **ROOKIE OF THE YEAR!**

He was the **first Australian** to ever win that award – what a

**LEGEND!**

NBA
ROOKIE
OF THE
YEAR

# LEGENDARY GAME

## WHAT?

2018 NBA season

## WHO?

Philadelphia 76ers vs
Cleveland Cavaliers

## WHERE?

Philadelphia, Pennsylvania

## FINAL SCORE?

132–130 to Philadelphia 76ers

## Why was it LEGENDARY?

Ben made **27 points, 15 rebounds** and **13 assists,** and bested LeBron James in an **EPIC triple-double showdown!**

'He's a student of the game. He wants to be great.'

LeBron James

# First All-Star Season!

In his **second season** with the Sixers, Ben shone again.

MORE **triple-doubles.** More **legendary stats.** Incredible **PASSING, SCORING** and **DEFENDING.**

**2000 points**

**1000 rebounds**

**1000 assists**

in just 125 games!

In January of 2019,
Ben received an
All-Star
selection
for the first time -
the first
Australian
to ever receive
this honour!

‘**Support from Australia** means everything because just being Australian, every time I put on a jersey, I know **I’m not only representing my family, but Australia** at the same time.’

**BEN SIMMONS**

# AUSTRALIA'S RICHEST ATHLETE!

In **2019,** Ben signed a deal to stay with the **Philadelphia 76ers** for **five more years.** His **talent** was so

by then, that the **76ers** agreed to pay him...

This deal made Ben

# AUSTRALIA'S RICHEST ATHLETE!

What would YOU do with all that money?

Buy some sweet sneakers and some cool art?
Buy a house or two? Or three?
Buy your mum something nice?

# BEN'S LEGENDS

Ben collects the jerseys of other **legendary athletes,** including:

**Magic Johnson**

**Chris Paul (CP3)**

'One of my **favourite athletes** of all time, he's just incredible at what he does at **such a high level.**'

BEN on Lionel Messi

## Or you could make a...

# MOVIE

Ben is the executive producer of the documentary

***The Australian Dream.***

It's about legendary AFL star **Adam Goodes** and his **activism in fighting racism,** on and off the sporting field.

'It's a great documentary and it's going to open up a lot of doors, for not only **multicultural kids** but **Indigenous kids**... My dad is from **America** and I'm a **mixed kid** growing up in **Australia**, so I felt like I owe it to the other kids who have **been in my situation.**'

**BEN SIMMONS**

Even legends have to deal with **losing** and form **slumps** sometimes. In **2021,** Ben was not having a great time in Philadelphia.

His shooting was off, he seemed to lack some of his usual confidence, and the **Sixers were losing games** they thought they should win. **Ben thought it was time for a change.** He wanted to be traded to **another team.**

# NOTHING BUT NETS

BAGELS

In **February 2022,** Ben was traded to the **Brooklyn Nets.**

Brooklyn is in **New York** - an exciting city full of amazing **art galleries** and **restaurants, music** and **theatre, bagels** and **pizza**...and subway **rats.**

Since joining **the Nets,** Ben has had some serious **injuries** that needed **surgery,** which has kept him **off the court** a lot.

It can be **frustrating** to be on the **sidelines** when you desperately want to play.

But when you are an **elite athlete,** it's really important to look after your **body** and your **mental health.**

**In fact, that's really important no matter who you are!**

**But real legends shine when things get difficult,** and Ben has been working hard to make it back to his best. Since his return from injury, he has been **making his mark** at both ends of the court with...

**Elite defence**

**Driving to the basket**

**Dunking**

**Genius passing**

Brilliant team play

And a TRIPLE-DOUBLE against the San Antonio Spurs – 10 points, 10 rebounds, 11 assists!

**Aussie fans** might be secretly hoping that Ben will choose to come home and **play AFL,** but it looks like he might be on his **way back to his NBA best.**

# AUSSIE AUS

Ben **hasn't represented Australia** since his Under 17 World Cup days. Everyone was hoping he would play for **the Boomers** at the **Paris Olympics in 2024,** but sadly injury has ruled him out.

'The storm doesn't last forever. I'm going to get back to where I was. Each day is a day to get better.'

**Ben Simmons,** in 2024

First overall draft pick

36 career triple-doubles

First Australian to win NBA Rookie of the Year

Selected to play in the All-Star Game three times

Australia's highest-paid athlete

Most points by an Australian in an NBA game

There is no doubt: **Ben Simmons** is a true

***SPORTING LEGEND!***

1. Where was Ben Simmons born?
2. What sports did Ben Simmons play as a child before focusing on basketball?
3. Ben won a scholarship to which high-performance sports training facility?
4. Which NBA team drafted Ben Simmons as the first overall pick in the 2016 NBA draft?

**5.** What position does Ben Simmons primarily play in basketball?

**6.** Ben Simmons attended which university before entering the NBA draft?

**7.** How tall is Ben?

**8.** What is the name of the Australian national basketball team that Ben Simmons has represented in international Under 17 competitions?

**9.** Ben Simmons is a triple-double legend! What three categories are triple-doubles usually made of?

**10.** Name one of Ben's nicknames mentioned in this book.

**ANSWERS:** **1.** Melbourne, Australia **2.** Rugby and AFL **3.** Australian Institute of Sport/AIS **4.** Philadelphia 76ers **5.** Point guard **6.** Louisiana State University (LSU) **7.** 2.08m **8.** The Boomers **9.** Points, rebounds and assists. **10.** Benny, The Wizard of Oz, Fresh Prince or Big Ben

**Alley-oop:** When you throw the ball towards the basket, and your teammate leaps up to catch it and dunk it in one motion.

**Bank shot:** When the ball bounces off the backboard and into the basket.

**Splash:** When you make a three-pointer from far away.

**Euro-step:** To do this, pick up your dribble, take a step in one direction, and then quickly take a second step in a different direction. Let your defender try to catch you now!

**Granny shot:** When you shoot the basketball underhand.

**Fadeaway:** This one takes skills! It's when you make a jump shot while falling backwards away from the basket.

**Dagger:** A shot (often a three-pointer) that typically occurs in the last moments of a game and seals a win for a team.

**Air ball:** A throw that doesn't come close to making it inside the basket. Yikes!

**Brick:** Another type of missed shot! Here, the ball hits the metal rim of the basket or the backboard before bouncing off.

**Dropping dimes:** When you assist/pass the ball to other players on your team in a way that helps them score easily. It comes from the phrase 'dropping a dime', which refers to the cost of a payphone when you're assisting the police with a tip on someone.